To Dino   E.P.
To M.M. and I.M.   D.K.

Text by Elena Pasquali
Illustrations copyright © 2005 Dubravka Kolanovic
This edition copyright © 2005 Lion Hudson
Artist commission and design by Jacqueline Crawford

The moral rights of the author and illustrator
have been asserted

A Lion Children's Book
an imprint of
Lion Hudson plc
Mayfield House, 256 Banbury Road,
Oxford OX2 7DH, England
www.lionhudson.com
ISBN 0 7459 4914 2

First edition 2005
1 3 5 7 9 10 8 6 4 2 0

A catalogue record for this book is available
from the British Library

Typeset in 18/24 Caslon Oldface BT
Printed and bound in Singapore

Ituku's Christmas Journey

Written by Elena Pasquali

❄

Illustrated by Dubravka Kolanovic

LION
CHILDREN'S

Little Ituku sat outside his snow house. He always liked to watch when the magic lights streamed across the northern sky.

'The lights are shining from heaven,' said Ituku to his faithful dog, Jaq. 'We're so lucky that they shine all the way to earth.'

Jaq gave a little howl to show he agreed.

As the two watched, the ribbons of colour parted. A yellow shape uncurled in the sky.

Ituku gasped, and Jaq crouched down, growling.

The yellow shape became a giant polar bear, with eyes of midnight blue. It lowered its head closer to Ituku and Jaq.

'Do not be afraid,' said the bear. Its voice was deep but very
gentle. 'I bring you good news. The king of heaven has been
born on earth. You must go and look for him.'

Then the bear vanished back into the sky, and the ribbons of
light swirled in a merry dance.

As soon as the sun rose, Ituku packed his kayak. He needed
food and water for his journey. He did not know where
he was going or how long the trip might be.

'Come, Jaq,' he said. 'Take your
place on the front of the deck.
We will go together.'

Ituku set off, paddling bravely among the glittering icebergs.
Whales came and flipped their tails as if to say goodbye.
Wide-eyed seals swam by and stared. They seemed to want
to know where the boy and his dog were going.

Soon Ituku's kayak was being swept along in an ocean current. Jaq felt the cold air whistling past his ears. Ituku pulled his hood closer. He had never travelled so fast.

As evening came, they saw a land with snow-covered hills. Ituku paddled his kayak to a pebbly beach. He and Jaq found a sheltered hollow and huddled there to camp.

A snowshoe hare came tiptoeing out and stared at them.

Jaq wanted to bark with excitement; but he remembered to be polite and only uttered a tiny squeal.

Soon, more and more snowshoe hares crept out shyly.

'May we rest here one night?' asked Ituku. 'We are travelling to find the king of heaven.'

The first hare nodded, and then all the hares scampered away. In the night, when Ituku and Jaq were fast asleep, they came tiptoeing back. They snuggled around the boy and his dog to keep them warm.

The following day Ituku and Jaq paddled on, the kayak
skimming swiftly across the water. In the evening, the bright
glow of a fire led them to another shore.

'I hope your dog knows how to behave himself,' said a gruff
voice. In the shadows sat a group of shepherds. Nearby, their
sheep jostled and bleated.

Jaq sat down obediently. Ituku spoke to the shepherds. 'We are
travelling to find the king of heaven. Is he here?'

'Not here,' replied the men, 'but we've heard of such a king. Shepherds in a faraway land say that angels told them where to find him. If the story is true, you've a long way to go.'

The following morning, Ituku and Jaq set off again. 'I'm feeling tired,' said Ituku to his dog. 'I wonder how far we have to go?'

All at once, a brightly painted fishing boat came sailing towards them.

'Hello!' called a boy. 'Do you want to come aboard? We can pull your boat behind us.'

'Yes please,' said Ituku, and Jaq wagged his tail.

An orange cat was sleeping on the deck. It opened one eye, winked at Jaq and then snuggled back to sleep.

'We are on a journey to find the king of heaven,' explained Ituku.

The boy swung the sail and smiled. 'Where I come from, we tell stories of a king from heaven who will be a friend to fishermen. I hope you find him.'

The wind carried them all the way to the boy's village. The people gave them a warm welcome: delicious food to eat and soft beds to sleep in.

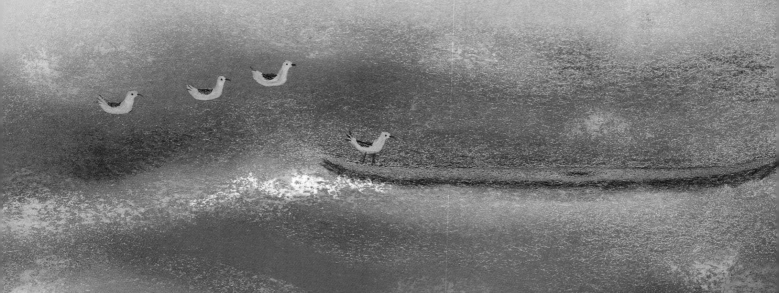

'Good luck!' cried the boy, as he watched Ituku and Jaq paddle on the next day.

The air was warmer now, and the sea was calm. A land that was the colour of gold shimmered in the sun. Ituku and Jaq saw people and camels travelling in a long line.

'Let's stop and ask them about the king,' said Ituku. He found a beach where the road came close to the sea; but the men and the camels had turned in another direction.

Ituku shivered as the sun set. The air turned cold. A thin sliver of moon appeared in the sky.

A desert fox trotted by. Jaq sat up, ready to defend Ituku. The fox sniffed and stopped to look at them.

'I have a hole to go to,' he said. 'Don't you have a place to go?'

'No,' replied Ituku. 'We are travellers. We are looking for the king of heaven.'

'Ah, that explains it,' said the fox. 'The king of heaven doesn't have a home on earth either.'

He trotted away.

In the dark of the night, an owl hooted eerily. Mice
skittered over the sand. Jaq closed his eyes and tried to
shut his ears, but he couldn't sleep. Neither could Ituku.

He watched the sky as the stars came out. He knew them all,
and how they travelled across the night sky.

Then he blinked. There was a new star, brighter than he had
ever seen before.

'It's beautiful,' whispered Ituku. 'It must be a special star.
Come, Jaq, let's paddle closer.'

They set out across the silverlit sea; but the star seemed to
be travelling on… further and further.

When the day dawned, Ituku was too tired to paddle any more.
'I'm going to find somewhere to land,' he said.
He could just feel the sand beneath the kayak when, all at once,
a pack of dogs came racing towards them. They
splashed into the shallow water, snarling.
Behind them came soldiers, weapons
at the ready.

'You… you in the boat! Do you know anything about a newborn king?' shouted one.

Ituku was about to answer, but Jaq simply stood up and howled. Then he turned and barked at Ituku.

Ituku understood. He paddled off as fast as he could.

Later that day, Ituku let the kayak drift. 'We have no more food,' he said to Jaq. 'Stay very quiet while I catch some fish.'

When the hold was full, Ituku made his way into a sheltered cove. He could see people outside a cave. The man swung a lantern to welcome them.

'May I use your fire to cook my fish?' asked Ituku. 'I have some to share as well.'

'Of course,' said the man. 'I am Joseph, this is Mary, and here is our new baby, Jesus.'

All at once, Ituku knew he was looking at the king of heaven. He stood there in wonder. Jaq came as close as he dared. The baby laughed for joy.

Ituku shared the fish he had caught; the little family shared their bread and wine.

The next day, Joseph and Mary and Jesus travelled on.

Ituku and Jaq set out for home. 'Wherever we go, we must tell people that the king of heaven has been born,' said Ituku, 'so they will be able to go and find him. Then they will be able to share a simple meal with him, as we have done.'